Lucy Freegard

PAVILION

Poppy came from a long line of performers.
Many skills had been passed down
from penguin to penguin.

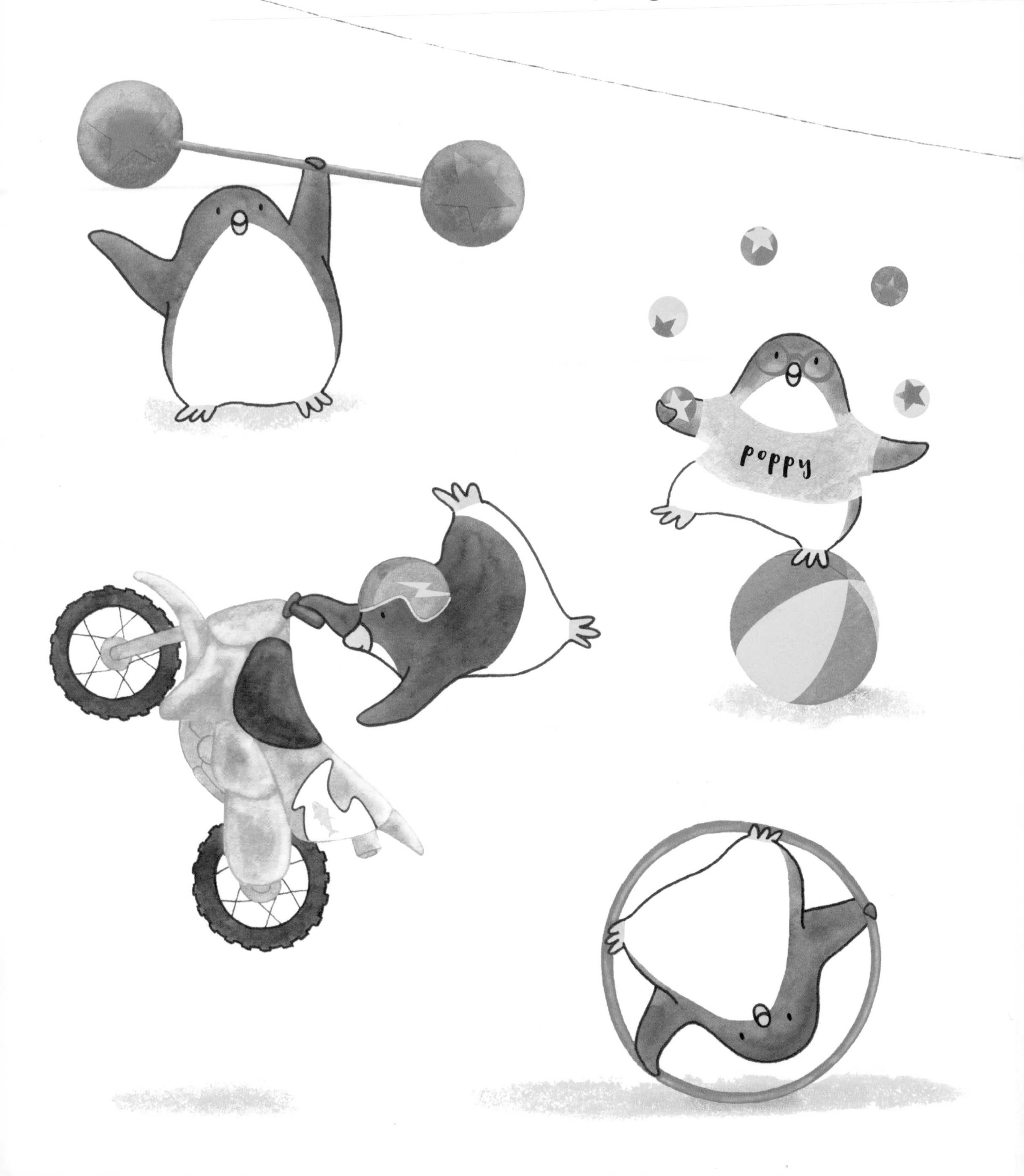

From a very young age, Poppy had taken part in her family's shows.

She made magic with
her mum. The audience
adored her!

Every week the penguins
travelled from town to town
to perform their amazing show.

And every day, they trained together.

Even lunchtime became a juggling act.

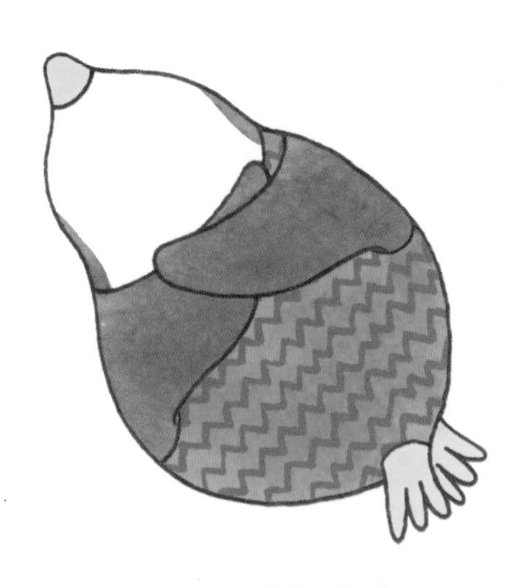

It often took months to master their moves.

All Poppy wanted in the world was to make her parents proud.

So she threw herself into the trickiest of tricks.
And before long...

Ooo...

Ahh...

Ooo...

Ahh...

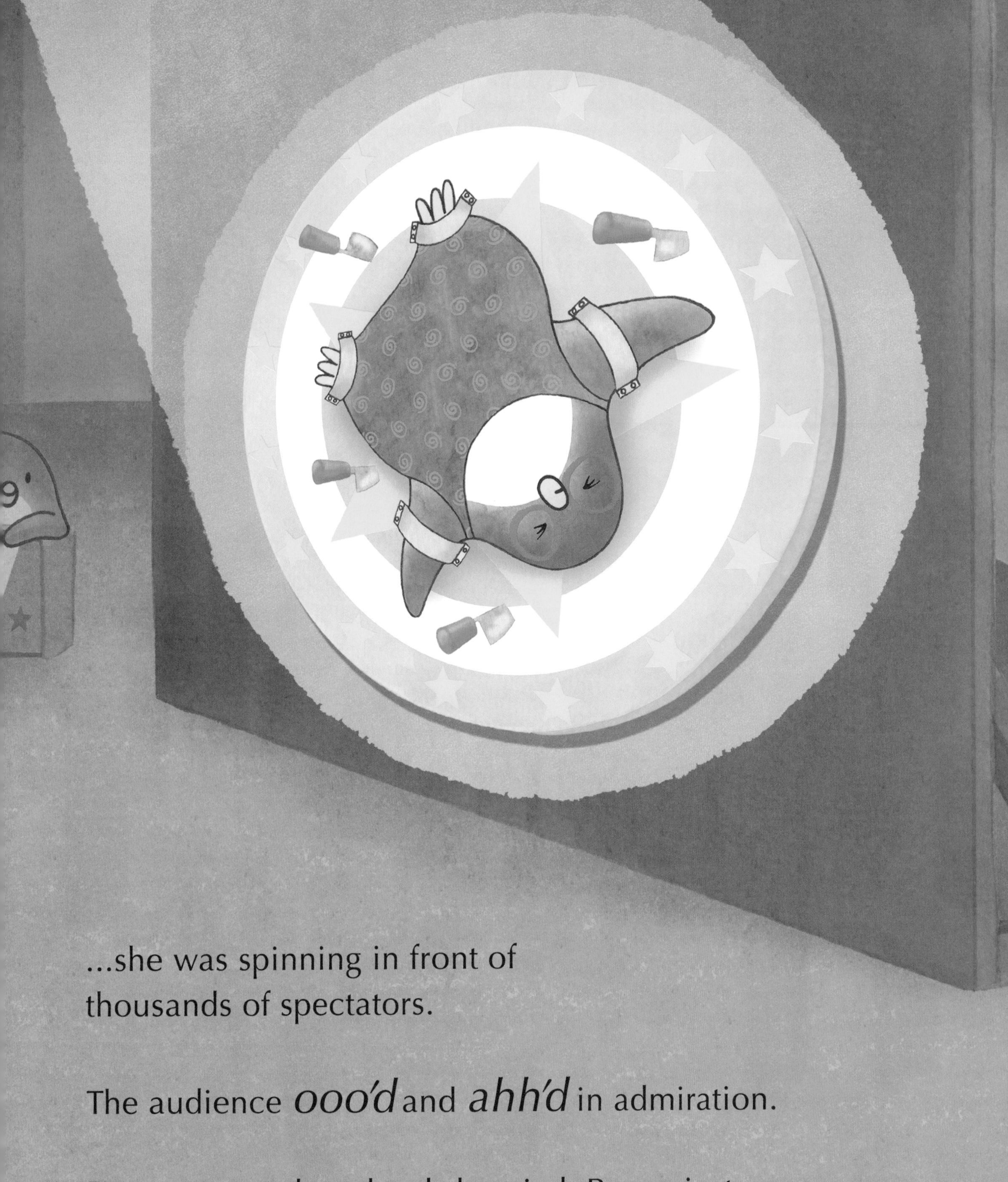

...she was spinning in front of
thousands of spectators.

The audience *ooo'd* and *ahh'd* in admiration.

But no matter how hard she tried, Poppy just
wasn't enjoying herself.

Deep down, Poppy knew that performing wasn't her passion. She didn't like loud noises, bright lights or crowded places.

Instead, she preferred to feel calm…
…and in control.

One night,
Poppy couldn't
pretend any more.

"Maybe I'm not cut out for this," she thought.

But her biggest fear wasn't falling off the trapeze, breathing fire, or riding a unicycle.

It was telling her mum that she didn't want to perform any more.

"We all need a little peace and quiet sometimes," said Mum.

After a while though, Poppy had a peculiar feeling.

She missed the costumes.
She missed the music.
And most of all, she missed...

...the magic.

Then Poppy had a brilliant idea.
Rather than performing in the show,
she would help to run it.

She began by
holding auditions
for new acts.

“This is going to be the greatest show ever.”

Next, Poppy had to master some new skills.

She learnt about lighting.

She painted some props.

She created
new costumes.

During the performances, Poppy made sure that the penguins were in the perfect place at the perfect time.

She finally felt calm and in control.

And, best of all...

...she was able to peek through the curtains and watch the greatest show on earth.

Together, the penguins charmed the crowds.
Everyone had a smile on their beak.

Especially her parents.
They were so proud of their calm, quiet Poppy.
She had become...

...the Greatest Showpenguin!